orever

The Against the Odds Saga

J. Adams

J. Adams

II

Forever

The Against the Odds Saga

J. Adams

J. Adams

Forever

V

To the fans who have love Raine and Hayden as much as I do.

Thank you!

$\mathcal{T}$ightening the wool sweater around me against the evening chill, I sit down on a metal folding chair, allowing my gaze to take in the familiar surroundings, and wait for Hayden to come. I expect him any time now and he is never late. There are children running around a nearby playground, chasing each other through the trees, mothers pushing their young ones on the swings and catching them at the bottom of the slide. The picture is one of perfect serenity and makes me smile. Staring off into the distance I take in the view of the sunset, marveling as I have so many times before at the colors, and deeply ponder life and how fragile and short it is.

I am sixty-five now, yet at times I still feel twenty-five inside. At other times I feel older because of the experiences life has thrown my way. Yes, some things have been hard, but I can't help feeling equally grateful for the bitter and the sweet moments of my life because of the growth they have, and still do bring.

Thanksgiving is two weeks away and I spent a good part of the morning writing a Christmas list. Twenty-one grandchildren to buy for! It's still hard for me to believe sometimes that we have so many. And there are two more on the way. As usual, our house will be full on Thanksgiving day, and the laughter of our adult children and their spouses will ring through the air, adding to the joy their presence brings. I am looking forward to having everyone close again. I just hope I can get everything done.

"Hey," comes Hayden's deep voice as his warm arms enfold me.

"I'm so glad you made it," I say, closing my eyes.

"Me, too, darlin'," he whispers against my ear, rubbing his stubbly face against my cheek. He shaved his beard off years ago, the same time he cut his hair, but his soft whiskers help me not miss it so much.

"How has your morning been?"

"Busy."

"It seems like life just keeps getting busier for us, but I cherish these times with you. I *need* them. You know that, don't you?"

He kisses my brow. "I do know." Sighing, he holds me close. "So, where are your thoughts right now?"

"Oh, on different things, but mainly on the kids coming for the holidays."

"But you're thinkin' about one Thanksgiving in particular." The statement is spoken softly.

I smile, a melancholic sadness filling me. "Always."

One

Fifteen years ago.

"Shelly is leaving. She wants a divorce."

"Oh, Dane, I'm so sorry."

Moving to the sofa, I embrace my son. He presses his face to my shoulder like a lost child and my heart aches for him. Hayden and I have expected this for some time, but it is still a shock to hear.

Dane met his wife, Shelly, at a friend's party a little over a year ago. Having moved to Roswell from New York just two months before, Shelly had been unsure about staying. Meeting Dane changed that.

Theirs had been a whirlwind romance that produced a hasty wedding after only two weeks of dating.

After getting to know Shelly better, I soon came to the conclusion that leaving New York and the comfortable life her parents provided had been an act of rebellion on the part of the twenty-year-old debutante, and the life of a rancher wasn't what she thought it would be.

Dane's hopeless love for her had been obvious. Now it seems his feelings for her had been far deeper than hers for him. Sadly, Hayden and I could see it from the beginning. Dane couldn't. Then she began accepting phone calls each day from a male 'friend' in New York, which marked the beginning of the end.

"What can I do, Mama? I don't know what to do."

I draw back a little, studying his anguished expression. Though his plea sounds like that of a little boy, in some ways this whole ordeal has aged him and he is like an old soul in a younger man's body. A foot shorter than his father, Dane is lean, muscular and very attractive, inheriting his handsome features from Hayden. He also inherited his father's kind heart and ability to love unconditionally. Any woman would be fortunate to have him and count herself blessed.

Any woman, that is, except the one who should. And now she is ripping his heart apart.

"I don't think there is anything you *can* do, Dane. I've watched you turn yourself inside out for her. You have given and given and she has done nothing but take. You even offered to go back to New York with her, but she didn't want that, either. You have sacrificed so much of yourself that you aren't even *you* anymore." I stop speaking as a wave of paternal emotion rolls over me. "It hurts us so much to see you going through this. I know you are in more pain than we can possibly grasp, but we hurt for you just the same."

Smiling brokenly, he reaches out and wipes the tears trailing down my face, and then his own. "I do know, Mama. And I know it's gonna be hard, but I'll manage somehow." He sighs. "I ain't got much choice in the matter, right?"

Taking his face in my hands, I press a kiss to his brow. "You will get through this, and we will always be here for you," I tell him. "Always."

7

"I know. And I thank ya for that."

* * *

Hayden

Having finished brushing the last of the horses down and emptying the feed bucket, Hayden hangs it on the stall hook and closes the door, all the while thinking on the trials that have beset Dane. Hayden truly feels for his son.

How well he remembers the day Dane and Shelly announced their engagement. Hayden and Raine had been concerned about this very thing happening one day. He remembers Dane saying, "I'm just following in my daddy's footsteps." Dane had thought he and Shelly would have the kind of love his parents had. And maybe they could have.

But there was one major difference:

Shelly wasn't Raine.

Taking a seat on a wooden bench outside the stall, Hayden allows his thoughts to travel back through the years to the day he allowed his fear of Raine one day growing tired of ranch life and wanting to leave come between them. Emotionally, that mistake had cost them both dearly.

Many years ago.

Hayden and Raine were sitting on a blanket, each holding a cup of lemonade, when she began to tell him about an earlier phone call. She told him about the major modeling job offer with her old agency in Atlanta and what she had already decided. Through her entire explanation, he hadn't said a word. He just stared out over the lake. When she finished, he finally looked at her.

"So, why didn't you tell me this morning?" he asked her, holding inside thoughts and emotions he hated himself for, but was unable to stop from feeling.

"I didn't say anything because I had already made up my mind. I don't want the job."

He heaved a deep sigh, pushing a hand back through his tousled hair. "Well, at least now I know what was wrong when you came out earlier." The way she'd acted when she ran out to meet him told him there was something she wasn't telling him. He had come to know her that well.

She hurried on. "Hayden, listen to me. Really listen. My mind was made up as soon as she asked me. There was no question as to what I would say." She touched his arm and he fought the sensation of longing her hands against his skin normally produced. "My life is here, with you." She took his hand in hers. "You are the most important thing in the world to me."

"That's a lot of money, Raine. You sure you can turn it down just like that? I mean, you must have at least considered it." He watched her tuck a spiraled lock of hair behind her ear, wanting more than anything to run his fingers through the dark tresses. He loved it when she wore her hair down.

"Truthfully, I was flattered. No, actually flattered is an understatement. I was seriously thrown for a loop to be made such an offer. But I was never tempted."

He tossed a pebble out across the water, hating the part of himself that couldn't believe her. "Still, you didn't tell me. I feel like you were purposely keeping it from me."

"I wasn't keeping anything from you." He could hear the frustration in her voice. "Hayden, please don't accuse me of something I'm not guilty of. I love you and I would never try to keep anything from you. It just wasn't important to me. If I had truly been considering it, believe me, you would've been the first to know."

He drew his legs up and wrapped his arms around his knees. After a couple of moments of agonizing silence and *internally fighting what he was about to say, he gave up. "I don't wanna hold you back, Raine. I don't wanna be the reason you give up that kind of money."*

"You're not holding me back. Give me a little more credit, will you? If I had wanted the job, I would have taken it. But I didn't." Stubbornly, he said nothing and he could tell she was getting angry.

"When I really want to do something, Hayden, no one will keep me from doing it."

"What's that supposed to mean?" He could feel anger rising inside him as well.

"It means that I love you and I don't want to leave, and no amount of money or position will make me leave. I don't need it, and I don't want it. I only want you." She paused. "You're what I need."

Hard as he tried not to, he felt himself softening a bit. Then she moved closer and touched his face. "I love you, Hayden."

I love you, too, baby, *he thought.* I love you so much, and that's why I have to do this.

"Please don't push me away. I didn't do anything wrong and I don't deserve this."

Latching on to that statement, he turned to her then,

keeping the hard look in his eyes. "No, you don't deserve this. You deserve better, a lot better than me." He stood. "Call them back and take the job, Raine. We can call everything off." The shocked and hurt look in her eyes pierced his heart and nearly undid him.

"What do you mean?" Her voice cracked. "What are you saying?"

"I mean I'm not gonna stand in your way. You deserve a lot better than me and this kind of life. You can have better if you go back."

He saw the threatening tears in her eyes, but he knew she was too strong to let them come. She stood and moved to stand in front of him.

"This isn't about money, Hayden and you know it. I don't need money. This is about you pushing me away. I don't know why, but you are. You said you loved me. You said you wanted to marry me more than anything. Have you changed your mind? Are you having second thoughts? Are you suddenly scared to make the commitment? I mean, it's like . . . like this is your way of getting out of marrying me, of getting rid of me."

He groaned inwardly. No, baby, that' ain't it at all. *He said nothing, he just continued to look out over the lake.*

You don't understand. I just can't stand the thought of losing you. And I know I will. Eventually, I will. *If only he had the courage to tell her that. But he couldn't speak the words.*

After a few moments, he watched her eyes narrow slightly as she looked up at him. Then she snorted, completely surprising him.

"So, I guess you've dabbled in a little brown sugar and decided you'd rather go back to white. The new flavor has lost its excitement. Is that it?"

Ouch! *He winced.* "That's not how it is with me, Raine. You know that."

"I thought I knew you. I thought I knew you better than anyone, but I guess I was wrong." *She pressed her palm against her forehead and shook her head.* "I can't believe this," *she muttered under her breath.* "You know, in some ways you're no different than Jerome."

Oh, now he was angry! How can she even think that about him? "Woman, don't you dare compare me to him! I would never cheat on you or treat you the way he did!"

"No, you wouldn't cheat on me, but you sure know how to make me feel the same way he did!"

And he did. He had sworn he would never hurt her.

He promised. Yet here he was, doing exactly that. And he couldn't seem to stop.

"Oh, I'm fine to make out and get your kicks with," she continued, *"maybe even eventually sleep with, but not good enough to commit to."*

"That's not true, Raine." His voice broke slightly. "I could never use you that way. I just think this is for the best."

"What's for the best exactly? Telling me you don't want me before you end up stuck with me? Is that what you mean?" She took a deep breath and pressed her lips together tightly. She suddenly looked so tired, so worn. And it was his fault.

He watched her silently empty the cups and put them back in the basket. Then she picked up the blanket and folded it. "Take me back, please."

He closed his eyes and sighed. Damn, damn, damn you, Hayden! *"I never meant to hurt you, Raine."*

"I'm done talking. Just take me back."

Like the coward he was, he dropped Raine off and left a few days later–on their supposed wedding day, to be exact– not telling her he was leaving or when he would be back. When he'd stopped by Caroline's to say he would be gone for a while, he'd hoped he would get a glimpse of Raine because he already missed her so much it hurt, but she was napping. Instead, he got a verbal whipping by his sister-in-law and was called the Biblical term for a donkey before driving off.

Every moment Hayden was away from Raine was torture, and he had been able to deal, barely, until the day he called home and was told by Caroline that Raine wasn't there, and that they didn't know where she was. His heart hammering madly, he jumped in his truck and drove all night to get back, kicking himself for being such a jerk and praying the entire way that she would be there, that he hadn't lost her.

And thanks to the good Lord, he hadn't. She was still there. He found her in his home, curled up on the sofa, sleeping softly, waiting with the precious gift of forgiveness and unconditional love. He hadn't deserved her then. But he was determined to make himself worthy of her.

Hayden knows he is fortunate to have married a strong woman–a woman who had loved him more than anything, and still does. Still, he would rather Dane had experience the pain he himself had felt back then than this terrible heartache his son is going through now.

Moving into an empty stall, Hayden closes the door and kneels to pray for Dane, hoping with all his heart that his son will have the strength to make it through this.

Two

*T*he next day I walk down to the barn to talk to

Dane, stopping just outside the door when I hear Shelly's voice.

"I'm leaving now. My flight isn't until tomorrow, but . . . I think under the circumstances it's best that I stay at a hotel tonight."

When I don't hear Dane respond, I peek inside. His back is to her, and though he is standing as still as a statue, I can make out the slight trembling of his shoulders. There is only one other time I've seen that stance and it was when I accidentally overheard a conversation between the two three months ago.

We went to Las Vegas for a family vacation. As soon as we hit the strip, Shelly had squealed, saying, "Now this is my kind of town!" She dragged Dane from one end to the other, missing nothing. By the time we got back home Dane was exhausted. We hadn't been home a week before she began nagging at Dane to go back. Approaching their open bedroom door, I heard them arguing.

"Why can't we go back? There's so much to do there, not like this hick town."

"Shelly, we just got back and I have work on the ranch. I can't just pick up and go."

"Damn the work, Dane. You don't need to stay here. We can afford to go anywhere we want."

"I have responsibilities."

"Well, I don't."

"Shelly, if you can just wait a few months I'll take ya back."

"That's too long. Besides, the other workers can handle your share of the work."

"It's not their job to do my work, it's mine."

"You are being ridiculous!"

"We can't go right now."

"Dane, one of these days I just might be gone and you'll be sorry you were so stubborn."

With that, Shelly exited the room. Shock filled her expression when she saw me standing in the hallway. Dropping her eyes, she rushed past me. I glanced in the room at Dane. His back was turned, but his shoulders were trembling.

She hurt him badly that day, and every day since.

How can she do this to my son? The heartless little . . .

"I never meant to hurt you," she continues. "I just know I could never have made you happy."

Dane's sigh is resigned. "You never tried."

"I did try. I just . . ."

"Save it, please, Shelly. I don't wanna hear anymore. You've already pretty much messed up my world so there's nothing left to say. Just . . . just leave, okay?"

I watch her move to touch him, then stop before turning to leave. She finally walks out, glancing at me as she come through the door. She stops but doesn't say anything. She can barely meet my eyes.

Taking one last moment to study her wavy blond-in-a-bottle hair, large blue eyes and porcelain skin that has remained untouched by the sun–mainly because she's spent most of her time indoors–I utter a single sentence before heading into the barn.

"You never deserved him."

* * *

After comforting Dane for a bit and making sure he is okay–well, as okay as he can be at the moment–I go in search of Hayden, holding my emotions inside as much as I can until I find him on another part of the property checking the newly-weaned calves. The moment his arms are around me I crumble.

"Hayden, he's hurting so much," I sob.

"I know, darlin'. I know."

"I can't believe she's doing this to him."

"We knew she would eventually."

"She should have tried harder. She could have been happy here."

"She isn't you."

"He deserved better."

"And hopefully one day he will have better."

Every parent harbors high hopes for their

children. You dream of them growing up to be great people, that they will have a fierce love of God and family, that they will marry well and raise their own family well. Yet you also understand and accept that so many things can happen to them, some far worse than others. I try to remind myself of this as I think of Dane. Regardless, it is still hard to watch him grieve for a life with someone that was never truly his. I also remind myself that Dane's life is in God's hands.

"It's gonna be all right," Hayden murmurs into my hair.

I finally draw back a little and smile, drying my tears. "I know. And thanks." Pressing a hand to his cheek, I caress the soft stubble. "I love you."

"And I love you." He kisses me then, stoking the usual heated passion between us as his warm mouth makes thorough work of claiming my very breath, giving me his own, and heating me to the core.

"Better?" he breathes, softly nibbling my bottom lip, his tongue lightly grazing.

"Yeah," I answer breathlessly. "But now I have a different need."

"I think I can take care of that." His voice is low

and seductive.

In a matter of minutes we are home in out room. Wrapped up in one another, our passion rages like the wind-tossed sea. Whenever I am emotionally broken inside, there is always Hayden's love. There is nothing it can't fix. And I don't think that will ever change.

Raising up, I gaze at his perfect form, chuckling at the sexy grin splitting his face. "Remember our first year of marriage and how we couldn't keep our hands off each other?"

"You know I do," he drawls, pulling me down and granting me another taste of his sensuous mouth.

"I thought some things would slow down with age, but I guess I was wrong."

"I guess so." He caresses my back. "But you don't mind being wrong about that, do ya?"

"Not at all," I happily admit, molding myself against him for a final few moments of bliss.

After lying in each other's arms for a while longer, we finally get up and dress. The twins will be back soon and I need to get dinner started. It has been years since they came into our lives, and we can never thank God enough for blessing us with those two, and we will be forever grateful to their biological mother for finding us worthy enough to raise them after she passed away.

Sixteen years old now, Liesl and Kurt have finished home schooling and now help out twice a week at Maggie's place, which is an hour away. Liesl helps tend her one and two-year-old niece and nephew while Kurt gives Maggie's husband, Lance, a hand with outside chores. Maggie and Lance's home is a large fixer upper. They have been renovating it for the past six months and it is coming along nicely. Lance has lived in Roswell all his life and we know his family well. He is a good man and we love him dearly. An attractive man, he is Native-American, which Maggie declares is the reason all their babies will be beautiful. I just shake my head every time she says this. Her sense of humor definitely makes her her daddy's girl.

* * *

Dinner tonight could be a solemn occasion, but the twins won't allow it. They have always had a way of bringing joy to the lowest of souls and Dane is no exception. He has never been able to resist Liesl and Kurt's charms and this evening they are in rare form.

With Liesl going on about what a catch he is and how the women of Roswell will freak when they find out he's back on the menu, and Kurt's assurance that some of his own female friends will age faster just to have a chance at his big brother, there is just no way Dane can keep a straight face. Yes, I can still make out the underlying sadness in his gray eyes, but I can also feel the lightness of his heart, if only for a moment.

Three

We spend the following week preparing for the coming Thanksgiving holiday. Maggie and her family will be here, as well as Dave and Caroline's son and his family, so we will be having the big dinner at the main house.

Dane has stayed busy, working with his dad around the ranch, and except for the slight sadness in his eyes at times, he seems to be doing better. But his efforts don't fool me. I know he is still hurting and will for a long time. We've had a few late night talks, and he and Hayden have as well. We do our best to assure him that we will always be here for him and are always willing to be a listening ear whenever he needs a sounding board.

* * *

Hayden

Having spent most of the day repairing fence lines on another part of the property, Hayden and Dane talk as they put the tools away.

"Sometimes I still feel so lost. And I never imagined I could feel so alone. It's harder than I thought it would be and . . ."

When Dane pauses, Hayden notices the shift in his expression. "What is it, son?"

"Daddy, I . . ." He swallows, grimacing as if he just tasted something bitter. "This morning I was getting rid of some stuff Shelly left and . . . I found a piece of paper with a couple of numbers on it. Don't ask me why I didn't just throw it away, but I didn't. Instead I called the numbers."

"And?" Hayden presses when Dane hesitates.

"They were the numbers of two guys. No one answered either of them, but the voice mail recordings were men." He shook his head, rubbing his eyes. "I don't know why I was surprised. She did take off into town every now and then. She always said she just needed to get out for a bit. Now I know where she was *getting out* to."

"I'm sorry, son." Hayden doesn't know what else to say. Infidelity is something he has never given a thought to in his marriage. He and Raine have always been completely devoted to one another and he knows that won't ever change. He has no experience in that area and feels ill-equipped to offer Dane advice.

"Sometimes I wonder if it's even worth it anymore."

"If what's worth it?"

"Living."

Hayden swings around to face his son, shocked and angered to hear him say something like that. "Let me tell you something, Dane. Every breath you take on this earth is worth it, and you should be damned grateful for them. You have no idea what your mama sacrificed to bring you into this world."

He takes in Dane's startled expression at his vehemence, glad his words had that effect. Swearing again under his breath, Hayden's thoughts go back to Dane's birth and what Raine went through. He'd almost lost her that day, and he can't imagine anything more painful than losing her, or seeing her suffer in any way.

Hayden echoed the doctor's command telling Raine to push. It only took a few hard pushes to bring their son into the world. At that moment, he experienced a joy that could not be defined. He was finally a father. He now had a son by the woman he loved more than life. They both laughed and cried, and Hayden kept kissing her, telling her how proud he was of her. They emotionally gazed at their son when the doctor placed him in Raine's arms.

"He's so beautiful," she whispered.

"He is," Hayden said against her face. "And so are you."

She turned and kissed him. "I love you."

"I love you too, baby."

"Let's get this little guy weighed," Dr. Salem said. Raine begrudgingly handed little Dane back to the nurse. Hayden couldn't blame her for not wanting to let him go for a minute.

The doctor came over and rested a hand on her

shoulder. *"You did great, Raine, really great. But I honestly haven't seen a first time birth happen that quickly in a long time. And believe me, that was quick."*

Hayden grinned, squeezing her hand. *"I guess he was anxious to get out here and see the world. He's just like his mama."*

When Raine tried to smile, Hayden realized something was wrong. The right side of her face suddenly began to twitch. He watched her eyes move from him to the doctor, then back to him just as her body began to seize, and his heart literally stopped that very moment.

"Raine!" he frantically called. *"Raine!"*

Dr. Salem had the nurse take Hayden out and he paced back and forth in front of the door, determined to not leave that spot until he knew Raine was okay. Every second he had to wait was agony.

Later, he sat beside the bed holding his wife's hand, wiping the tears streaking his face. It had been hours since their son came into the world. Hours since the powerful seizure shook Raine's body, causing her to lose consciousness. Hours since he had been gifted with the teary gaze of her beautiful brown eyes.

Raine was in a coma.

When Doctor Salem had finally come out and given Hayden the news, he had immediately asked how it happened and why. "When will she wake up? Will she even wake up?" He had struggled with the doctor's straightforward answer.

"I don't know. All we can do is wait."

Wiping his face once more, Hayden moved closer to the bed and laid his head against his wife's shoulder, fingering a curl lying against the side of her face, and softly spoke to her.

"I'm here, darlin'. I'm right here. And I ain't going nowhere." His emotions bubbled to the surface again. "You gotta wake soon, baby. I need you. So does our little boy. We need you so much, Raine."

Raising his head slightly, he gazed at her face. "Come back to me, baby. Please come back to me." Pressing his face back to her shoulder, the tears began anew.

It was a nightmare, one he couldn't seem to wake up from. His beautiful, sweet wife might be taken from him. They hadn't even been married a year, and he could lose her. He couldn't bear the thought.

Surely God hasn't brought us this far to take it all away.

The pain was threatening to tear him apart. If he had

been a drinking man, he knew he would be sitting in the corner of a bar somewhere completely wasted, trying to numb the pain. But if he did that, he wouldn't be where he should be. He wouldn't be at his wife's side, being the kind of man and husband she deserved. Not that he felt he really deserved her anyway. He'd tried to be worthy of her, though, and if she made it through this–when she made it through this–he would try even harder.

Later that afternoon, Caroline and David brought Hayden a couple of changes of clothing and his toiletry items. There was no way he was going to leave the hospital without Raine and they knew it. He cried in their embrace and accepted the comfort they offered. He had asked them to call Raine's mother, which they did. They told him she would be flying in the next day.

A while later, the nurse brought little Dane in to Hayden and he held his son for a long while. He talked to Raine the entire time about their baby. That evening the same nurse brought him a pillow and blanket to use in the recliner when he was ready to sleep. He didn't think he would be able to, but once he slid the recliner as close to the bed as possible, he eventually gave in to exhaustion and drifted to sleep with Raine's name on his lips and a prayer in his heart that he wouldn't lose her.

A week later she came back to him, and he counted himself the most blessed man in the world.

"Son?" Hayden finally says, his thoughts returning to the present, his stare intent. "I know you're hurtin', but don't ever say anything like that again. Don't even think it. All right?"

"All right, Daddy. And I'm sorry."

Four

Awakening just before dawn, I snuggle closer to Hayden and he wraps his arms around me.

"Happy Thanksgiving," comes his deep voice, raspy with sleep.

"Happy Thanksgiving." I burrow deeper into him. "I need to get up, but . . . you're too warm and cuddly for me to leave."

"Cuddly, huh?" His lips brush my brow.

"Uh huh, like a big teddy bear."

"But a little less furry."

"A little."

He grins and I know I am in for it. Sure enough,

he begins tickling my ribs and I jump up, but he catches me before I can make it out of bed.

"Hayden!" I try to keep my voice down. "Let me go."

"Why?"

"Because I need to get up."

"You mean you need to get away from me."

"That, too."

"I thought so." He renews his assault and I'm locked in a fit of giggles. Then he slowly kisses me and our activity merges into something entirely different and far more enjoyable.

An hour later I finally make it out of bed to get ready for the day. Standing in front of the bathroom mirror, I stare at my reflection, taking in the unmistakable marks of my age. Bits of gray streak my hair and a few laugh lines are visible around my eyes. If the modeling industry still had its claws in me, those two features would be considered problems and quickly remedied. A good dye job and a few Botox injections are the fashion industry's cure-all, and I would most likely have had a few sessions by now. As for my body, it is still passable. Barely. To the world, anyway.

Peering deeply, I search for signs of the twenty-six-year-old young woman Hayden fell in love with. She is in there, I know, because I glimpse her from time to time. I still catch her smile and the alluring tilt of her head every now and then. She is still there, she's just layered with life's experiences and aged like a fine wine, each passing year adding more value, thanks in part to my husband and children. They have each had a hand in shaping me, and I hope I have done my very best with the whole mother thing. I know nothing is ever perfect–including me–and it is both impossible and unrealistic, but I still want the best for my children. I want them to marry the best people and live the best lives–not free from trials, but in spite of them.

And with all my heart, I want this for Dane. He deserves a fresh start and another chance at happiness. This, more than anything, is my fondest wish for him.

Hayden appears behind me and I smile as his arms circle my waist, his chin nuzzling my shoulder. Like most handsome men, he grows even more handsome with age. Gazing at our reflection, I heave a deep sigh. We do still look great together.

"What do you see when you look at me, Hayden? Answer truthfully."

"When do I not?" Just as I open my mouth to comment, he adds, "Wait, don't answer that." I smile, giving him my signature arched brow.

Tightening his embrace, he rests his head against mine, staring into the mirror. "What do I see when I look at you? I see the woman who stole my very breath the moment I looked up and saw her standing in the barn with Caroline. I see the woman who charmed a quiet old man and an even quieter younger one into opening up and talking more than they ever have to a woman that wasn't related in some way." He turns me in his arms and looks into my eyes intently. "I see the woman who was, and still is, the most beautiful thing I had ever seen. The woman who became my best friend before our first roll in the hay." I snort and he grins. "And if we'd stayed in there any longer, the hay bales would've spontaneously combusted and the whole place would've gone up in flames."

"But that night in the bed of your truck was even hotter."

"You got that right. The view of the moon was

never more beautiful–what we saw of it, anyway." His expression turns serious. "I see all those things each and every time I look at you. But mostly, I see the woman I love more than anything in the world, the mother of my children, my soul mate, and the keeper of my heart. You will always be everything to me, Raine."

"And you will always be everything to me," I say, drawing his head down and kissing him passionately. "Thank you."

"You're welcome."

"You know what I see when I look at you?"

"Darlin', you show me what you see every time you touch me, or even look at me."

"If we had a little more time I would show you even more." He groans at my seductive smile.

"You're killin' me, honey. But I guess that gives me something more to look forward to at the end of the day."

J. Adams

Five

*G*rabbing a platter of vegetables and a large basket of rolls from Caroline's counter, I take them to the dining room and place them on the long table with the rest of the food. Everyone is here and the house is full. Grandchildren-both Caroline's and mine-run to and fro, the older ones trying to keep up with the younger ones. This is what I love most about the holidays. Having family together brings me great joy.

Throughout the afternoon, I watch Dane interact with the family. He laughs a lot and really seems to be enjoying himself. Though things have been hard for him, he is better than he was. I think being surrounded by people who love him helps.

After a second grazing of the dessert table, all the adults head out for a game of horseshoes while Liesl and Kurt push Maggie and Lance's little ones, Devin and Crystal on the swings in the small playground beside the house. Caroline's grandchildren join them. We adults usually get pretty loud when competing in horseshoes and today is no exception. Hayden and I make a good team, and never ones to give up, we usually play until either we have won the most games or blisters become too painful to play any longer. The latter doesn't happen often.

Dave gets a ringer and Hayden knocks it off, which starts a brotherly argument between the two. Dave says Hayden should have pity on him since he is so much older and cut him some slack. Hayden says Dave should stop playing the age card and just 'suck it up.' Then comes the silly routine of playfully harassing each other about things they did when they were young. And finally, the muscle-flexing competition comes. As usual, we are all shaking with laughter because they are so thoroughly entertaining. After a few minutes of this, the game resumes.

Scanning the yard at one point, I don't see Dane. When ten minutes have passed and he hasn't reappeared, I ask Hayden to take my final turn and I go in search of him. Checking the first floor of the house, there is no sign of him and I head upstairs. I find him sitting in the guestroom I stayed in when I first came to live with Caroline and Dave. His back is to me and he is facing the window.

"Dane." He doesn't respond and I go to him. "Dane, what is it?"

He finally looks up at me through anguished eyes. "What is it?" I ask again, sitting down next to him. When he finally speaks, his voice is raw with emotion.

"Shelly called me. She said she was pregnant, but . . . she lost the baby."

"Oh, Dane!"

"I asked her how she knew it was mine. She called me a jerk and hung up."

"I'm so sorry." I tearfully squeeze his hand, my heart aching for him yet again. This news is devastating and I can only imagine what he must be feeling.

"It was a stupid thing for me to ask," he says,

looking down.

"She gave you reason to wonder. Anyone in your position would."

"Daddy would never had said something so hurtful."

"No, but I've never given him cause to. And he has never given me cause to worry. Although there was one time when I briefly experience the pain of wondering. But even then, my small moment of worry was pointless."

Dane's eyes met mine. "You worried about Daddy cheating?"

"No, I trusted your father completely, it was the hoochie home wrecker hussy I didn't trust."

He smiles a little at my choice of words. "What happened.?"

"Well, when I was pregnant with you and confined to bed rest, your daddy had to make a hay delivery to the home of a woman who never seemed to grasp the concept that he was a married man and had no desire to associate with her in any way. He felt bad about having to make the delivery and I hated the thought of him going, but he had no choice and I accepted that it was his job."

Thinking back on that day, I share the experience with my son.

It was almost dinner time when Hayden finally came through the front door. I had missed him terribly, even more so than normal. I looked up as he entered the bedroom. He smiled, but it didn't seem to reach his eyes.

"How are you doing, baby?" he asked, leaning down to kiss me.

"I'm okay." My voice belied what I felt inside. I was happy he was home, but at the same time I wanted to ask him why he hadn't come to me before now. "How did things go today?"

He slipped the dirty t-shirt over his head, sat on the edge of the bed, and pulled off his boots. "It went fine," he finally answered, not looking at me. He headed to the bathroom.

My heartbeat sped up a little. It wasn't like him to be so quiet. Not around me, anyway.

"Hayden?" I said, just as he was entering the bathroom. "Is . . . is everything all right?"

Smiling, he came back over and kissed me again.

"Everything is fine, darlin'." And without another word, he went to shower.

I squeezed my eyes shut, determined not to let my imagination run away with me. I trusted Hayden. If he said everything was all right, then I would believe him.

He was unusually quiet that evening. He was loving and attentive as always, but something was wrong. I knew it deep in my soul. Something had happened. It wasn't until he undressed and got in bed that I finally gathered the courage to bring the subject up. Inside I was still nervous. Actually, I was scared to death he would tell me something I didn't want to hear.

"Hayden?" I said as he reached over to turn off the lamp. He paused in his actions to look at me, the wariness in his gray eyes increasing my uneasiness.

"Yeah, darlin'." I hesitated and he said, "What is it?"

I looked at him for another moment without speaking. Suddenly everything I had planned to say completely left my mind. "Talk to me, Hayden." The wary look in his eyes grew. "What happened this morning? And don't say nothing. You promised to be completely honest with me and I promised you the same." I lifted a hand to his face and he immediately squeezed his eyes shut. "Talk to me."

He finally opened his eyes and I was startled as I witnessed a mixture of anger and sorrow sweep through them. Tears began to sting my own eyes. "Hayden, please. Don't leave this to my imagination. I have already done that enough today."

Tears filled his eyes. He gently caressed my face and it was another full moment before he spoke. "I'm so sorry, Raine," he finally said.

"About what?"

His bottom lip began to tremble. "I just feel so ashamed." He paused, looking into my eyes. "That's why I didn't come back by today. I went straight to work because . . . I couldn't come home yet, Raine. I felt ashamed."

By now hot tears were streaking my face. "Ashamed of what?"

He silently stared at me for a moment before speaking again. There was so much pain in his eyes, I feared what he was about to tell me. I found myself bracing for his words, a familiar ache creeping inside me.

"Never in my life have I ever hit a woman. I never let myself get that angry before. But today . . ."

My heart was hammering, but for a different reason now. I pressed a hand to his face, caressing his beard. "Tell *me what happened, Hayden. Nothing you tell me will change my feelings for you. I promise."*

He took a deep breath, his eyes pleading for understanding, which I was determined to give to him. "As soon as I got to her place and started unloading the hay, she came out." He grimaced, as if it pained him to even think about her. "Just like I expected, she started right in on me marrying you. She said a lot of things I don't care to repeat, and some things that aren't worth repeating. I got angry and told her to go back into the house and leave me alone. I said a few other things too that I probably shouldn't have." He stopped and looked away.

I sat up a little and took his face in my hands, urging him to look at me. "Tell me, Hayden. Tell me everything."

He gently pulled me back down, wrapping me tightly in his arms. "I'm so sorry, Raine. I didn't mean to do it, but I was so angry . . . and she wouldn't leave me alone."

"It's okay. Just tell me."

He took another deep breath. "When I opened the door to get back in the truck to leave, she grabbed the front of my shirt and tried to kiss me. She said . . . she said she could satisfy me in a way you couldn't. And I . . ."

"You what?"

"I pulled her hands from my shirt, but she grabbed me again. I . . . I finally shoved her away from me and she fell. I flung her like a rag doll, Raine, and she fell hard. She hit her head."

He paused, wiping his eyes. "I felt awful. I was about to tell her I was sorry and ask if she was all right, but she jumped up and started yelling, calling me every name in the book. Then she started in on you again. I finally got in the truck and left. If I had stayed there any longer . . . I would've really hit her, Raine. I know I would've. I've never completely lost my temper before. I can't believe I did it." He closed his eyes and turned away.

"Hayden, look at me. You didn't do anything wrong. It was just a reflexive action that made you shove her. I know the situation is different, but I had the same reaction with Chris when he kissed me. I know you well enough to know you would never purposely hurt anyone, especially not a woman. In fact, you champion women more than any man I've ever seen. She was trying to provoke you and you handled it the best you could. You didn't do anything wrong."

"Baby, please tell me you don't think any less of me for . . ."

I quickly took his mouth with mine, silencing his words, trying to take his pain into myself, and his response was immediate. He pressed me close and hungrily accepted my comfort.

"I love you more than anything else in this world," I finally whispered against his lips."Don't ever doubt that."

"I'm just sorry to bring this on you now when stress is the last thing you need. I'm supposed to be taking care of you, not making things worse."

"Shhh. You are taking care of me. No one has ever loved and cared for me the way you do. You're the best man I've ever known."

He held on to me tightly. "I love you."

"I love you too."

"Wow," Dane finally whispers. He gives me another sad smile. "Daddy is a good man."

"And so are you."

"I wish I could live up to him."

"You don't have to. Don't even try. Your daddy is your daddy and you are you. Trying to be like him is fine, but don't try to *be* him because you are an amazing man just the way you are."

"But not enough for Shelly, I guess."

"Dane, don't feel guilty over this. I know you loved Shelly deeply. She hurt you by leaving. Last week you found evidence that she was unfaithful, then out of the blue she calls and announces that you were going to be a father, but you aren't now. That's a lot to take in in such a short time. And none of it is your fault." I pause, squeezing his hand again. "You may not believe it now, but there is someone out there for you, Dane. Someone who will deserve your love and give you that same love in return. Just allow yourself time to heal and get through this. The pain will eventually pass. And I know this is all easier said than done, but it will be okay. I promise."

"How can you be so sure?"

"Because I've been there, remember? Even though the situation wasn't the same and I didn't really love my ex husband, I did care for him and his infidelity truly hurt, at first. But by the third time I was done. I felt nothing for him, I just wanted out. When I came to Roswell I wasn't looking for love. But your daddy blew into my life and that was it." I pause, touching his face. "Just give it some time. You will heal and your heart will open again one day. All right?"

Saying nothing, he simply nods. Wrapping my arms around him, he rests his head against my shoulder and silently accepts my comfort. I wish I could read his thoughts right now, and though the mother in me wants to pry his feelings out, I don't try. I just silently vow to be there for him.

Six

Standing *beside Dane's crib, I quietly watch him*

sleep. The rise and fall of his chest fills me with peace. He is a
beautiful baby and I can already tell he will someday be big
and strong like his daddy. He has Hayden's eyes and his
smile. Like all mothers, I dream of his future and all he will
accomplish. I see him out riding horses and working around
the ranch, charming a girl with his handsome grin.

I turn away from the crib a moment and then turn
back. The scene has changed and he is now a man. The two of
us are sitting at the kitchen table.

"I can't do it, Mama."

"Do what, honey?"

His tear-filled eyes are intent, his voice pleading. "I love you and Daddy."

"We love you, too, Dane."

"I can't do it."

"Do what?"

He answers me, but I can't hear him. His mouth is moving, but his voice is silent. I can no longer feel his hand on mine. Then he begins to slowly fade away.

"Dane! Dane, come back!"

Awakening with a jerk, I glance at the clock. It is two in the morning, and my heart is pounding like a drum, a nameless dread descending upon me. It comes from nowhere and clouds my thoughts and emotions.

"Hayden."

"Hmmm?"

"Something's wrong."

"What is it?" He awakens fully.

"I don't know, but . . ."

I have no idea what drives me, but I get up and automatically head down the hall and run up the steps, coming to a stop at Dane's bedroom door. Hayden is right behind me, gripping my hand. Not bothering to knock, I just open the door.

"Dane," I call softly, slowly moving toward the bed.

He doesn't answer.

Heart threatening to beat through my chest, I turn on the bedside lamp. "Dane?"

He is lying on top of the blanket completely still. Lifting a trembling hand, I touch his hand and then his forehead, finding both cold.

"No, Dane!" I cry hoarsely, a river of tears flowing down my face, my insides ripping in two. "Baby, no!" I turn to Hayden just as he drops to his knees, an empty pill bottle in his hand and a note that simply says, *I'm sorry* in Dane's handwriting.

"Why, son?" Hayden whispers. "Why?"

Sitting on the bed, I lift Dane's head, placing it in my lap, my soft cries turning to wracking sobs, the pain in my heart so profuse, I want to die, too. Hayden holds Dane's hand to his chest, rocking back and forth, a painful howl tearing from his body. The sound only serves to increase my own agony.

"Oh, my baby!" I continue to wail, holding his head against my heart. "My baby."

The twins rush into the room and immediately

begin to cry, calling out Dane's name, crowding close.

Hayden finally calms enough to call the paramedics. As he talks, I futilely ask myself why I hadn't checked on him before going to bed. With all my heart and soul I wish that I had. How alone he must have felt, and how desperate.

I'm so sorry, Dane. I'm so sorry you felt so alone.

Hayden hangs up the phone and we wait. Liesl and Kurt crawl onto the bed and scoot as close to their brother as possible.

None of us move again.

* * *

Three days later.

Sitting in the front row facing Dane's casket at the cemetery, I stare straight ahead through puffy eyes–the result of non-stop crying–and return the comforting squeeze of Hayden's hand as I contemplate the day.

Getting out of bed the past few mornings was a challenge, and today was even worse. Yet somehow I managed. I think the reason today is much harder than I anticipated is because I know that in the next ten minutes, Dane's casket will be lowered into the ground and that will be the end of his chapter of this life. Our son will be gone and we won't see him again until we join him in death. And oh, how that knowledge hurts right now.

I glance around at our family, their sad expressions increasing my own sorrow. Everyone adored Dane and a large hole is left in his absence, one that will never be filled. He had been everything to everyone. Everyone except the person that had mattered most to him.

My eyes briefly move to Shelly sitting apart from the family. There is no point in placing blame, nor will I waste the words. She is in her own private hell and the result of its dark depths is etched into her features. When she showed up last night with tears streaming down her face, she could only manage, "I'm so sorry," but that was enough for Hayden and I to take her in our arms. She had come to the realization of what she'd lost–no, what she gave up–too late. She had hurt him badly. Now she will have to live with that knowledge.

Moving my gaze to Hayden now, I again squeeze his hand. He smiles, but his eyes are empty, his handsome face aged overnight.

After Dane's body had been taken away that

night and we'd spent some time with the kids, I lay on our bed holding Hayden in my arms for a long while. Neither of us have been so broken since the time I was attacked long ago. Back then, Hayden had something to take his anger out on. I was told later how it took three men to pull him off the worker that tried to rape me. Our friend Dean had gone back to the hospital to check on the man. Dean told us his jaw had been wired shut and he had a couple of broken ribs. It is assumed he left town after that. We never saw or heard from him again, which suited us all just fine.

The gentle pull of my hand draws me back to the present. Moving closer to Hayden, I rest my head against his shoulder, comforted by his lips against my brow.

The reverend says some final words, gives an internment prayer, and the service is over.

* * *

At the end of the day when everyone has gone, the twins go to bed and the house is quiet. Hayden and I lay in bed holding one another and my minds drifts into deep contemplation of the day.

How do you sum up a life of twenty-three years

in only a few hours? As I softly cry against Hayden's chest, I reach the conclusion that you can't. It's impossible–almost as impossible as it is to calculate how much that person could have accomplished, how many lives could have been touched for the better had he lived.

Part of me is angry–angry at Dane for taking the easy way out. I almost died giving him life, and for him to take his own life is a slap in the face that is almost as painful as losing him.

I am also disgusted at myself for being angry at all. No one knew what was going on inside Dane but him and the Lord. Judgmental thoughts have no place in me and are to be avoided.

If only he . . .

Wiping my face, I remind myself that pondering what could have been is never productive. It does nothing to help me or my family, so I will leave that train of thought and venture down another avenue. Instead, I will remember the great life our son lived.

I will always remember.

Seven

The next couple of weeks are filled with various raging emotions in the family. The twins vacillate between bouts of tears and moments of melancholy. They desperately miss their brother and it will take a long time for the pain of his absence to relent.

Maddie keeps busy with her family, but during the quiet moments, emotion overtakes her, making it hard to even function. Thank heavens for her sweet husband. He is able to comfort her when no one else can. She and Dane had been as close as a brother and sister can be, and healing for her will take quite some time.

Hayden is quieter these days. I spend most

afternoons with him no matter where he is on the property, whether out repairing the fence, checking on the animals, or working in the barn. He always needs me near and I'm okay with that because I need to be near him too. Something has shifted inside both of us. Nothing is the same, and I don't think it will ever be again.

Some afternoons we have gone horseback riding, never saying much, just soaking in the closeness we share. Always sharing the same horse, we take a blanket out to our favorite spot amidst a grove of trees on the far end of the property and lose ourselves in one another. Afterward, we hold each other and cry a little, sharing an ache that even our arms can't assuage.

Most nights we sit out on the back lawn, wrapped in a quilt, and gaze up at the stars, conversing a little, but mostly lost in our own thoughts.

Occasionally, I turn over in the middle of the night to find Hayden lying on his back, tears trailing back into his hair. Taking him in my arms, I comfort him with my words and body. He falls asleep with his head on my shoulder, murmuring my name and his love for me. For some reason, my moments of grief occur just as he is about to leave in the mornings. He takes my hand and sits with me curled up on his lap, kissing my tears away in reciprocated comfort.

These things become a pattern, and within a month's time, tumultuous emotional moments calm as we slowly begin to feel peace. Then one day we receive a letter from Shelly that reopens the healing wounds. Sitting on the porch swing, I read it to Hayden.

Raine and Hayden,

You will hate me for what I am about to tell you, but the guilt is eating me up inside and I need to tell you this.

I called Dane the day he committed suicide, and what I told him most likely sent him over the edge. I will hate myself forever for what my actions have caused. I didn't lose the baby, I had an abortion . . .

"What?" I whisper, my heart cracking all over again. I slowly raise my eyes to Hayden, not surprised to see the hard look in his. Squeezing his hand, I continue.

The day I found out I was pregnant, I also tested positive for HIV . . .

"Oh, no," I murmur, shaking my head, my mind

instantly connecting the pieces before another word is read. *Damn her!*

Swearing, Hayden stands, digging a hand in his hair. "She gave our son a death warrant and murdered our grandchild." His shoulders rise and fall as he releases a deep calming breath. "Go on and finish." He sits back down beside me and takes my hand, urging me to continue. I don't want to because of the additional pain Shelly's words are sure to bring, but I do finish the letter.

I told Dane I couldn't bring a baby into the world knowing it wouldn't live a full life. I then suggested that he get checked as soon as possible. The doctor said I've had the virus for a while and was certain Dane probably did, too.

I hurt him so much, yet he didn't even say anything. I don't think he could. He just hung up. I wanted to tell you everything before the funeral, but I couldn't. I'm a coward telling you this way instead of facing you. No apology can ever make up for what I have done. I know this. But for what it's worth, I am so sorry about everything. Dane was a good man and he didn't deserve what I did to him. I wish I could change what I've done, but I can't.

I won't ask you to forgive me.

I don't deserve it.

I fold the letter and move into his open arms. Closing my eyes, I listen to a dove cooing softly somewhere in the trees. After sitting for a while in silence, Hayden quietly says, "No one else ever needs to know."

I couldn't agree more.

J. Adams

Eight

Six months later.

Biltmore Estate, Asheville, North Carolina

Needing some time alone, Hayden and I have rented a lovely cottage for a week. Other than touring the massive grounds of the Biltmore House, purchasing souvenirs and taking a couple of drives through the city, we spend our time at the cottage, healing and reconnecting. Many of our conversations are the same.

Hayden sometimes feels like he failed Dane as a father, and he wonders if there was something he could have done to prevent our son from taking his life. I repeatedly try to assure him that there isn't a better father walking the earth. I also remind him that Dane had his agency, and as much as his actions hurt, we could never have taken his freedom to choose, no matter what.

Whenever I feel Hayden beginning to slip into moments of depression, I pull him back with my love.

We spend a great deal of time reminiscing and discussing our children and how much joy they bring us. We think back on family vacations and silly things the kids have done–and still do, realizing that each day we have been given with them is a gift. Ours has been a good life. We have so much to be grateful for and have been blessed with all we could ever need or want.

* * *

On our final evening I find Hayden sitting out on the front porch, deep in thought. Our surroundings are lush and green. There are wooded areas in the distance and a grove of trees sits behind the cottage. It's absolutely beautiful here. He slides over on the patio love seat and I join him. I notice his brow furrowing slightly. He lightly massages his chest.

"Are you okay?" I ask as he wraps an arm around me, pulling me close.

"Just a little indigestion from that big dinner you fed me, but I'm fine."

"Well, I didn't force that third helping on you."

"True, but I ain't about to let good food go to waste."

"You never do."

"Nope."

For a long while we sit in silence, just taking in the peaceful world around us. With my head resting against his shoulder, I press a hand to his face, running my fingers back through his graying hair, warmth spreading through me as his lips rummage my brow. Then his mouth is on mine and the heat becomes a steady burn.

His voice is raspy when he drawls against my lips, "Too bad we don't have the pickup. I could park in in them trees over there and make use of the back."

"I'm sure you could."

His eyes slowly close as he kisses me deeply. "Let's go on in. I wanna love on you a while."

"Sounds good to me," I breathe.

* * *

The night is long, but we fill it. We savor it.

We love.

We talk.

We love.

We talk more.

We love again.

"I love you," he murmurs as we become one a final time. "I love you so much, baby."

"I love you, Hayden."

And then there is silence. The essence of all we are fills the room, finally lulling Hayden to sleep. But before I allow sleep to take me, I let my thoughts drift over our lives once more.

And I remember:

The day I realized I was in love with Hayden.

As I lay in the hay in the stable, I looked up at him and my heart began to beat wildly, almost hammering through my chest. I could feel something happening between us. We wordlessly stared at one another when his gaze moved to my mouth. My breathing became shallow as he placed his hands on either side of me in the straw. When he slowly lowered himself against me and teased the corner of my mouth with a light kiss, I released a breathy sigh my lips parting slightly, and his whole mouth descended upon mine in an heated exchange.

A soft moan escaped me as his moist mouth claimed mine. His lips caressed and plied mine with burning affection. He pulled me tighter against him and I felt his heart beating madly. His mouth tasted like the strawberry he'd eaten. I wrapped my arms around his neck and pressed a hand into his thick hair. His beard was prickly against my skin, but I loved it. I loved him. *I fell in love with him the very day we met.*

The night he asked me to marry him.

"Raine." His gentle voice drew me from my pondering. He lifted my chin, looking into my eyes, his gaze intent."I love you, baby. I love you so much, and I want you to be my wife."

The softly spoken words brought immediate tears to my eyes. I hadn't told him I loved him yet because he had never said the words to me. But I had wanted to.

I pressed a hand to his bearded face as tears spilled down my cheeks. "I love you, too. And being your wife is what I want more than anything."

Our wedding night.

Hayden took my hand and we walked back to the bedroom. Standing next to the bed, he silently gazed down at me and I could read his thoughts almost as easily as I could read the love and desire in his eyes.

"I can't believe I really have you," he finally said. "I can't believe you're mine."

"I can't either."

"I have ached to have you for so long, to be with you like this."

"I have wanted you, too. More than you know."

He continued to gaze down at me quietly for a another minute before turning and pulling back the covers.

Looking up at him in nervous anticipation, I could tell he was a little nervous too. I turned my back to him, lifting my hair for him to undo the buttons on my dress.

"Raine," he breathed into my hair, taking my shoulders in his gentle hands and turning me to face him. "It's been a long time for me."

I kissed his hand. "That is the best wedding present you could ever give me. You are the love of my life, Hayden McKade. And you will be the last man I ever give myself fully to. I am completely yours."

"Woman, you completely own me, heart, mind, body, and soul. And you always will."

Then there were no more words between us. Staring

into each other's eyes, we undressed, slipped beneath the cool covers, and we loved.

I never dreamed a body could experience so many things at once. His every touch, his every kiss, and his every whispered word literally took me to another world. When we finally became one, I reached a plain that I never knew existed. And I was amazed.

I remember various important events. The births of Dane and Maggie. The time of healing after my hysterectomy. The nights I cried myself to sleep because I wouldn't be able to have more children, and the increased love Hayden showered upon me, validating my worth.

The day I was almost raped.

Hayden quietly picked the rest of the hay from my hair. Nothing was said between us, because there was nothing I could say, and I didn't think Hayden knew what *to say, either. But his being there for me was enough. I took his hand in mine and lightly touched the swollen knuckles, silently thanking God for the strength of those hands. Hayden let me lower his hand into the water, releasing a sigh of his own.*

Sitting in the bathtub, I held the small ice pack against my eye, knowing without even looking in the mirror that my face was a sight. A tear slipped down my swollen cheek at the thought.

"You're still beautiful," he said.

I lifted his wet hand to my lips. His hands had saved me. The bruised knuckles had inflicted pain on my behalf, and I needed the touch of those same hands to help me forget.

Emotion welling inside me, I looked into his eyes, finding the same emotion etched into his features.

"Make it go away, Hayden," I pleaded. "Please make the pain go away."

Helping me out of the tub, he wrapped a towel around me and held me close.

"I'll make it go away, baby." He covered the bruises on my arms with gentle hands. "I'll make it go away," he repeated against my brow, carrying me to bed. Once I was between the cool sheets, cradled in the warmth of his embrace, my body was the recipient of his loving and tender caresses, my mouth and swollen face were bathed in the healing balm of his kisses, and he truly did make it go away.

In his arms, nothing could touch me. With the melding of my body to his, for those precious moments, the pain faded into nothingness.

I ponder the day we met Joy and were gifted

with the twins.

"I prayed you here."

Hayden and I glanced at each other. "What do you mean, sugar?" he asked.

"I mean I prayed for you to come. I have cancer. I've had it for almost nine months and I've been grateful for each new day I have been given. But I'm afraid I don't have many more days."

"Oh, Joy," I cried brokenly. "Why didn't you tell us?"

"Because I wanted to get to know you first. I thought I would have a little more time. I . . . I need to ask something of you."

"What is it?" Hayden asked. "You can ask us anything."

"What I'm about to ask you is the very reason I prayed you here."

We turned as the door opened. I gasped and covered my mouth with one hand, squeezing Hayden's hand with the other.

"This is why I prayed you here."

Rick and Lynn entered the bedroom, each of them holding a sleeping baby in their arms.

"This little lady is Liesl," Rick said, opening the pink

blanket, exposing the adorable, one-month-old infant.

"And this handsome fellow is Kurt," Lynn said, opening the blue blanket covering Liesl's twin. "Our Joy is a big Von Trapp fan and considers The Sound of Music the greatest movie ever made."

"My idea of the perfect family," Joy said. She looked at Rick and Lynn and they nodded, handing one baby to me and the other to Hayden. "I needed a kind, loving couple who would be willing to take my babies into their hearts and home, and love them unconditionally. I know God has chosen you. Please say you will take them."

"But why us?" I asked softly.

"Because I prayed, and you came into the cafe. From the moment I saw your motherly smile, and then witnessed Hayden's love for you, I knew you were the couple the good Lord wanted to take my children and give them a loving home. Please say you will take them."

Hayden and I looked at one another, knowing our thoughts were the same. I turned back to Joy.

"It would be an honor and a privilege to care for your children as our own."

Tonight I remember every cherished memory.

And then I place them all in my mind's treasure box and snuggle closer to Hayden, drifting to sleep with a full heart.

Nine

The singing birds outside our bedroom window awaken me. Opening my eyes, I turn beneath Hayden's arm, caressing his muscular bicep as memories of last night send warmth coursing through me. I touch his face, surprised when he doesn't awaken like usual.

"Hayden," I softly say.

He doesn't answer.

"Hayden."

He doesn't awaken.

"Hayden!" I cry, shaking him. "Wake up, Hayden! Please wake up!"

Finally, his brow creases. When his eyes finally open, only half of his mouth turns up in a smile.

* * *

The present

Hayden's gentle voice draw me back.

"I love you, darlin'."

"And I love you."

Hearing someone close by, I look up, noticing an older woman standing a few yards away, stooping with a poinsettia plant. She turns slightly, smiling at me, and I smile back. Then I return my gaze to the two granite headstones before me, looking from the one with Dane's name etched into it to the one directly in front of me bearing his daddy's name.

"I've never been able to let you go, Hayden. When the series of strokes finally took you, I just couldn't say goodbye. And you've stayed with me through all these years. You always come to me. How?"

"Because God knows you still need me."

Groaning from the familiar ache, I breathe deeply, waiting for the pain to pass. "It won't be long now, will it?"

"No, darlin', it won't." I feel the sensation of his lips against my brow. "Treasure the holidays, baby. And I'll be right here with you."

"You'll stay with me to the end?"

"To the end. And forever."

Epilogue

Maddie

Mama seemed fine through Thanksgiving, but by Christmas, she was confined to bed as the returning cancer slowly ate away at her. She was on pain medication most of the time, but even when she was hurting she never complained. In her room, she was surrounded by her favorite things. Pictures of her and Daddy covered the walls, and a framed portrait of Daddy in his favorite gray hat and faded plaid shirt sat on her bedside table. The portable stereo on the dresser always played a CD of their favorite country love songs, and a few of Daddy's shirts that had been packed away were now used by Mama to sleep in.

Since she couldn't be up, we all took Christmas in to

her. Her bedroom stayed busy with activity. We opened presents, ate and played games there, and the younger grandchildren even napped there, wanting to stay close to their grandma.

Then, as the holidays faded away, so did Mama. She died peacefully in mid January, and I know Daddy was there to take her home. In fact, I think Daddy was always there. Before Mama died, she told me he never left her, and that she talked with him daily. Of course, I thought it was the imaginings of a dying woman still in love with her husband. Then I heard her sweetly whisper his name with her dying breath. And call me crazy, but I could have sworn I heard Daddy's voice answer back.

What do I think now?

I believe her.

About the Author

J. (Jewel) Adams stays crazy busy with her family and writing. She has written several books in different genres, mainly romance, and is also a motivational speaker to both youth and adult audiences.

She is on the last leg of home schooling her two youngest, and between that and conjuring up new ideas for her books, her brain cells are on overload most of the time. She and her husband Sean are the parents of eight children and grandparents to five and counting.

In her spare time (when she has any) she likes to curl up with a good book and a healthy stash of orange Tic Tacs. She and her family reside in Utah.

Jewel loves hearing from her fans, so if you would like to contact her to tell her how much you love her books or give her sympathy for the fried brain cells, contact her at jewela40@gmail.com

To check out Jewel's other books, visit her website at **JewelAdams.com**

And stop by her blog: **jewelsbestgems.blogspot.com**

www.ingramcontent.com/pod-product-compliance
Lightning Source LLC
Chambersburg PA
CBHW070532130626
46555CB00003B/1379